P9-DWI-362

Disney

Christopher Robin

The Little Book of POOH-isms

With help from PIGLET, EEYORE, RABBIT, OWL, and TIGGER, too!

Printed in the United States of America
First Hardcover Edition, July 2018
3 5 7 9 11 12 10 8 6 4
FAC-038091-19039
Library of Congress Control Number: 2017959437
ISBN 978-1-368-02589-8

Designed by Gegham Vardanyan

Visit disneybooks.com

Logo Applies to Text Stock Only

Disney

Christopher Robin

The Little Book of POOH-isms

with help from PIGLET, EEYORE, RABBIT, OWL, and TIGGER, too!

Disney PRESS
Los Angeles • New York

As told to Brittany Rubiano
Art by Mike Wall

CONTENTS

A NARRATOR'S INTRODUCTION

Dear Reader,

Over the years, I've had the privilege of following the adventures of a certain bear with a soft spot for honey, Winnie the Pooh—perhaps you've heard of him? He lives right here, in the enchanting Hundred-Acre Wood. And though he has been called a bear of "very little brain," I have found him to be full of wisdom, as well as fluff. Oftentimes his thoughts are made in the most thoughtful way one could think.

Indeed, we could all learn a lot from Pooh and his friends—from how to weather blustery days to tips for facing Heffalumps to ways to bounce toward the Important Things in life.

Here is a collection of some of their most cherished thoughts.

Take a look.

And enjoy.

ADVENTURES

CHRISTOPHER ROBIN: Come on, Pooh.

POOH: Where are we going, Christopher Robin?

CHRISTOPHER ROBIN: Nowhere.

POOH: One of my favorite places.

Adventures to Nowhere are some of the greatest.

"If it's not Here, that means it's out There."

—WINNIE THE POOH

Comforting words when one has lost something important, like a key or a sock.

“The Hundred-Acre Wood needs a hero . . . and I’m the only one!”

—TIGGER

Solo adventures are sometimes the best kind.

"I always get to where I am going by walking away from where I have been."

—WINNIE THE POOH

Quests are funny things that way.

"Hello, there. Are you on an **expotition**, too?"

—WINNIE THE POOH

You never know whom you might meet on your travels.

“Sometimes if I am going Somewhere and I wait, Somewhere comes to me.”

—WINNIE THE POOH

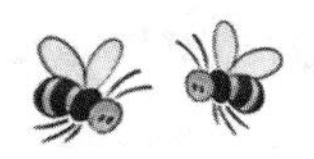

Somewhere is often just around the corner.

SANDERZ
RNIG
ALSO

"We keep looking for home, but we keep finding this pit. I thought if we start looking for this pit, we might find home."

—WINNIE THE POOH

The best path is not always the most obvious one.

"Oh, boy, it's good to be home."

—PIGLET

Coming home can be one of the nicest parts of the journey.

HUNN

LITTLE NOTHINGS and SOMETHINGS

"Doing Nothing often leads to the very best Something."

—WINNIE THE POOH

You never know what Nothing might bring.

CHRISTOPHER ROBIN: What I like best is nothing.

POOH: How do you do nothing?

CHRISTOPHER ROBIN: It's when people call out, "What are you going to do, Christopher Robin?" And you say, "Oh, nothing," and then you go and do it.

The best thing to do on a golden afternoon.

“People say nothing is impossible, but I do nothing every day.”

—WINNIE THE POOH

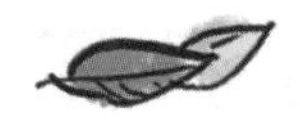

And twice on Windsdays.

HUNNY

"Sometimes the thing to do is Nothing. It often leads to the best Something."

—WINNIE THE POOH

And hopefully that something is honey.

FITNESS

“Ah, yes. Time to make myself hungry with my stoutness exercise.”

—WINNIE THE POOH

Morning routines can be useful.

"Guess I'm back where I started."

—EEYORE

Progress feels elusive, but don't let that get you down.

"Jump? Tiggers don't jump! They **bounce**."

—TIGGER

Do whatever is right for you.

“I’m not much of a bouncer.”

—EEYORE

Set your own pace.

HONNY

Up, down, up.

When I up, down, touch the ground,

It puts me in the mood.

When I up, down, touch the ground,

In the mood . . . for food.

—WINNIE THE POOH

It can be good to have a mantra.

HUNDRED-ACRE WISDOM

"You are braver than you believe, stronger than you seem, and smarter than you think."

—CHRISTOPHER ROBIN

Always remember. . . .

“Can’t change the inevitable, just have to go with the flow.”

—EEYORE

It might bring a nice change of scenery.

"It's worth a t-t-try."

—PIGLET

A good attitude is everything.

POOH: You must be catching a cold.

OWL: I'm not catching a cold. The word is "issue," not "achoo."

Gesundheit.

"Never trust that thing between your ears. Brains will get you nowhere fast, my dears. Haven't had a need for mine in years. On the page is where the truth appears."

—RABBIT

Hmmm . . . this could be what the Heffalumps and Woozles want you to believe. Best to keep reading and *thinking.*

"Think, think, think."

—WINNIE THE POOH

When in doubt . . .

"Thanks for noticing me."

—EEYORE

A little consideration goes a long way.

PIGLET: Don't you think today is just the right sort of day for a ramble?

POOH: I was just about to go somewhere, but I would much prefer a ramble. Because when you're going nowhere in particular, well, you are quite sure to get there.

Ramble on.

"If people are upset because you've forgotten something, console them by letting them know you didn't forget—you just weren't remembering."

—WINNIE THE POOH

Whoops.

"Ah, yes. I see it. Quite clear. Never really doubted it at all."

—OWL

It's okay to admit when you stand corrected.

HUNNY

“It’s good to try new things. Otherwise, how would you know how much you liked your old things?”

—CHRISTOPHER ROBIN

Lots of good reasons to try something new.

"A weather vane is not a Heffalump!"

—RABBIT

It can be hard to tell—always good to make sure.

W S N E
PLEZ CNOKE IF AN RNSR IS NOT REQID
PLEZ RING IF ANRNSER IS REQIRD

"I do like to keep things tidy. But I like visiting with friends even more."

—PIGLET

Both are important.

"You're welcome to have some thistles with me. If you don't mind the crunch, that is."

—EEYORE

Don't be prickly; share your favorite things.

HONEY

"I've got a rumbly in my tumbly."

—WINNIE THE POOH

Happens to the best of us.

"IOU an urgancee hunny pot."

—WINNIE THE POOH

Oh, bother.

"Hello, bee.
Oh, please tell me you have a hunny tree."

—WINNIE THE POOH

It never hurts to ask.

"Some things I tried made me more hungry, and some made me less hungry. But I'm afraid all of them made me think about honey."

—WINNIE THE POOH

We all get our cravings.

“Honey happens to be one of my **tummy’s** favorite colors.”

—WINNIE THE POOH

The tummy knows best.

"What could be more important than a little something to eat?"

—WINNIE THE POOH

It's always a good time for something sweet.

HUNNY

HUNNY

“The safest place to
keep honey from
Heffalumps
is in one’s tummy.”

—WINNIE THE POOH

The same applies to Woozles and Jagulars.

CABEGE

ORGANIZATION

"Make room for the real Important Stuff."

—TIGGER

Like bouncing and friends.

"That will be the Order of Looking for Things."

—WINNIE THE POOH

Always good to have a plan.

1. CHRISTOPHER ROBIN
2. HONEY

"Well, I am a bit bulky."

—EEYORE

You can always make room for a friend.

"I'll put it back with the other Important Things."

—WINNIE THE POOH

Important Things can come in all shapes and sizes. Just make sure you have a Very Important Place for them, of course.

HUN

BOTHERS (MUST BE WINDSDAY)

“There goes the tail. Typical.”

—EEYORE

But do not fear; things like tails tend to come back to you.

"Oh, stuff and fluff."

—WINNIE THE POOH

A stuck-y situation to be sure.

RABBIT'S
HOWSE

"All good gardeners know how to be patient."

—KANGA

But keep with it and you'll enjoy the haycorns of your labor.

“Don’t you worry. As my old uncle Orville used to say, worry is the way to concern. Or is it concern is the way to confusion? Or no, it was—”

—OWL

In any case, best not to get too caught up in the small stuff.

"I listened, but then I had a small piece of fluff in my ear."

—WINNIE THE POOH

No harm in asking to hear something again.

"Woke up. Windy. House blew down. Fell in the river. Can't swim. Just an average Windsday morning for me."

—EEYORE

Sometimes it really is just one of those days. Again.

"Too fast, too fast!"

—PIGLET

When things get overwhelming, just slow down.

"I'm not very good at having fun. Never quite got the hang of it somehow."

—EEYORE

Practice makes perfect.

"Tiggers only bounce up."

—TIGGER

A bounce in one's step helps immensely.

"You're either part of the problem or part of the solution."

—CHRISTOPHER ROBIN

Solutions are as plentiful as honeybees, haycorns, and found tails.

FRIENDSHIP

CHRISTOPHER ROBIN: I've changed tremendously.

POOH: Not right here. It's still you looking out.

A true friend always knows.

"It's so much more friendly with **two**."

—PIGLET

That goes for everything from shelf-reaching to smackerel-eating.

HUNNY

“Another good deed done, buddy boys.”

—TIGGER

It feels good to do good.

“It would appear that together or apart, we’re still the best of friends!”

—PIGLET

True friendships know no time or distance.

HUNNY

"How lucky I am to have such unique and wonderful **friends!**"

—Piglet

May we all be so lucky.

CHRISTOPHER ROBIN: Pooh, promise you won't forget about me. Not even when I'm a hundred.

POOH: How old shall I be then?

CHRISTOPHER ROBIN: Ninety-nine.

Forever friendships are the best sort.

TIME

HUNNY

"It's usually today."

—WINNIE THE POOH

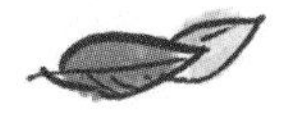

You can always check your Pooh-koo clock to make sure.

"Take your time.
I wasn't doing
anything important
anyway."

—EEYORE

It usually doesn't hurt to slow down a little.

"What's wrong with knowing what you know now and not knowing what you don't know now until later?"

—WINNIE THE POOH

Indeed, until the unknown becomes the known, best not to worry.

"Yesterday, when it was tomorrow, it was too exciting a day for me."

—WINNIE THE POOH

All in good time.

POOH: Christopher Robin, what day is it?

CHRISTOPHER ROBIN: It's today.

POOH: My favorite day.

Living in the moment at its finest.

BEING YOU

"Always be yourself."

—CHRISTOPHER ROBIN

Very Good Advice.

POOH: I don't feel very much like Pooh today.

PIGLET: There, there. I'll bring you tea and honey until you do.

Balloons help, too.

HUNNY

The wonderful thing about tiggers is tiggers are wonderful things. . . . But the most wonderful thing about tiggers is I'm the only one.

—TIGGER

Remember what's wonderful about you.

“Perhaps bears aren’t meant for such hard work.”

—WINNIE THE POOH

We all have our strengths and weaknesses.

ON WRITING

“I have asked him to propose a rissolution.”

—RABBIT

Rissolutions, poems, songs—all wonderful ways to express how you feel.

"T, I, double-guh, Rrrrr!
That spells Tigger!"

—TIGGER

A new meaning to "spelling bee."

"It's easier if people don't look while I'm writing."

—OWL

Quite true.

"One must be careful when decoding such arcane text so as not to incorrectly interpret its true meaning."

—OWL

Communication is key.

"One . . . thing . . . at a time."

—WINNIE THE POOH

It's all any of us can do, really.

"Ahem. 'Christopher Robin
is going.
At least I think he is.
Where?
Nobody knows.
But he is going.'
(I mean, he goes.)
'Do we care? We do. Very
much.
Anyhow, we send our love.
End.'"

—EEYORE

What a lovely poem!

WEATHER

"Have you ever happened to notice how many different colors the sky can be?"

—WINNIE THE POOH

Quite a lot.

“Easy come, easy go.”

—EEYORE

Weather is like that sometimes.

"I don't mind the leaves that are leaving. It's the leaves that are coming!"

—Piglet

Time to find a good rake, I'd say.

“When I say it’s going to rain, it always does. Sooner or later.”

—EEYORE

It doesn’t hurt to be prepared.

POOH: Oh, do you know where Winter is?

OWL: I can't say I do.

POOH: We'll have to hurry and find him.

The seasons will reveal themselves eventually.

"Can tiggers ice-skate? Why, that's what tiggers do the best!"

—TIGGER

With practice and a little help from friends, of course.

HUNNY

HIP HIP HOORAYS

"T-t-time for a celebration?"

—Piglet

To which the answer is always a resounding yes!

"Nobody could be uncheered by a balloon."

—WINNIE THE POOH

Always nice to have one on hand.

“If anyone wants to clap, now is the time to do it.”

—EEYORE

Sometimes people need a reminder.

“Come on, let’s bounce!”

—TIGGER

Another exceptional way to celebrate!

"It's my birthday, the happiest day of the year."

—EEYORE

And a good time for a happy surprise, I should think.

ENDINGS

"TTFN—ta-ta for now!"

—TIGGER

Good-byes just make for sweeter hellos.

"Good-bye?
Oh, no, can't we go back to page one and do it all again?"

—WINNIE THE POOH

Why, of course, Pooh. Just flip back to the start!

APPENDIX

Quote on page 11 from *Christopher Robin*, 2018

Quote on page 13 from *Christopher Robin*, 2018

Quote on page 14 from *A Hundred-Acre Wood Treasury*, 2011

Quote on page 17 from *Christopher Robin*, 2018

Quote on page 19 from *Christopher Robin*, 2018

Quote on page 20 from *Christopher Robin*, 2018

Quote on page 23 from *Winnie the Pooh and Tigger Too*, 1974

Quote on page 24 from *Christopher Robin*, 2018

Quote on page 28 from *Christopher Robin*, 2018

Quote on page 31 from *Christopher Robin*, 2018

Quote on page 32 from *Christopher Robin*, 2018

Quote on page 35 from *Christopher Robin*, 2018

Quote on page 39 from *Christopher Robin*, 2018

Quote on page 40 from *Winnie the Pooh*, 2011

Quote on page 43 from *Winnie the Pooh and Tigger Too*, 1974

Quote on page 44 from *Winnie the Pooh Storybook Collection*, 2012

Quote on page 47 from *Winnie the Pooh and the Honey Tree*, 1966

Quote on page 51 from *Pooh's Grand Adventure: The Search for Christopher Robin*, 1997

Quote on page 52 from *Christopher Robin*, 2018

Quote on page 55 from *Christopher Robin*, 2018

Quote on page 56 from *Winnie the Pooh*, 2011

Quote on page 59 from *Pooh's Grand Adventure: The Search for Christopher Robin*, 1997

Quote on page 60 from *Winnie the Pooh and the Honey Tree*, 1966

Quote on page 63 from *The Many Adventures of Winnie the Pooh*, 1977

Quote on page 64 from *Reflections in the Wood*, 2010

Quote on page 67 from *Disney's The Little Big Book of Pooh by Monique Peterson*, 2002

Quote on page 68 from *Christopher Robin*, 2018

Quote on page 71 from *Winnie the Pooh Storybook Collection*, 2012

Quote on page 72 from *Christopher Robin*, 2018

Quote on page 75 from *Eeyore's Gloomy Day*, 2012

Quote on page 76 from *The Sweetest of Friends*, 2011

Quote on page 81 from *Winnie the Pooh and the Honey Tree*, 1966

Quote on page 82 from *Christopher Robin*, 2018

Quote on page 85 from *Christopher Robin*, 2018

Quote on page 86 from *Better Than Honey?*, 2011

Quote on page 89 from *Reflections in the Wood*, 2010

Quote on page 90 from *Winnie the Pooh*, 2011

Quote on page 93 from *Disney's The Little Big Book of Pooh by Monique Peterson*, 2002

Quote on page 97 from *Christopher Robin*, 2018

Quote on page 98 from *Christopher Robin*, 2018

Quote on page 101 from *5-Minute Winnie the Pooh Stories*, 2017

Quote on page 102 from *Christopher Robin*, 2018

Quote on page 107 from *Christopher Robin*, 2018

Quote on page 108 from *The Many Adventures of Winnie the Pooh*, 1977

Quote on page 111 from *Friendly Bothers*, 2011

Quote on page 112 from *Christopher Robin*, 2018

Quote on page 115 from *Winnie the Pooh and Tigger Too*, 1974

Quote on page 116 from *Christopher Robin*, 2018

Quote on page 119 from *Christopher Robin*, 2018

Quote on page 120 from *Eeyore's Gloomy Day*, 2012

Quote on page 123 from *The Many Adventures of Winnie the Pooh*, 1977

Quote on page 124 from *Christopher Robin*, 2018

Quote on page 129 from *Christopher Robin*, 2018

Quote on page 130 from *Winnie the Pooh and the Blustery Day*, 1968

Quote on page 133 from *Pooh's Kindness Game*, 2018

Quote on page 134 from *The Sweetest of Friends*, 2011

Quote on page 137 from *A Portrait of Friendship*, 2011

Quote on page 138 from *Christopher Robin*, 2018

Quote on page 143 from *Christopher Robin*, 2018

Quote on page 144 from *Winnie the Pooh Storybook Collection*, 2012

Quote on page 147 from *Disney's The Little Big Book of Pooh by Monique Peterson*, 2002

Quote on page 148 from *Christopher Robin*, 2018

Quote on page 151 from *Christopher Robin*, 2018

Quote on page 155 from *Christopher Robin*, 2018

Quote on page 156 from *Christopher Robin*, 2018

Quote on page 159 from *Winnie the Pooh and the Blustery Day*, 1968

Quote on page 160 from *5-Minute Winnie the Pooh Stories*, 2017

Quote on page 165 from *Christopher Robin*, 2018

Quote on page 166 from *Winnie the Pooh and the Blustery Day*, 1968

Quote on page 169 from *The Many Adventures of Winnie the Pooh*, 2010

Quote on page 170 from *Winnie the Pooh*, 2011

Quote on page 173 from *Reflections in the Wood*, 2010

Quote on page 174 from *Christopher Robin*, 2018

Quote on page 179 from *Reflections in the Wood*, 2010

Quote on page 180 from *Pooh's Grand Adventure*, 1997

Quote on page 183 from *Winnie the Pooh and the Blustery Day*, 1968

Quote on page 184 from *Eeyore's Gloomy Day*, 2012

Quote on page 187 from *5-Minute Winnie the Pooh Stories*, 2017

Quote on page 188 from *Winnie the Pooh and Tigger Too*, 1974

Quote on page 193 from *Christopher Robin*, 2018

Quote on page 195 from *Disney's The Little Big Book of Pooh by Monique Peterson*, 2002

Quote on page 196 from *Christopher Robin*, 2018

Quote on page 199 from *Christopher Robin*, 2018

Quote on page 200 from *Disney's The Little Big Book of Pooh by Monique Peterson*, 2002

Quote on page 205 from *Winnie the Pooh and the Blustery Day*, 1968

Quote on page 206 from *The Many Adventures of Winnie the Pooh*, 1977